# THE MENTOR 2 - THE INFLUENCE GETS STRONGER

*A Cuckoldress Is Born*

## ALLORA SINCLAIR

Cuckoo
Publishing

THE MENTOR 2 - THE INFLUENCE GETS STRONGER

©2021 by Allora Sinclair

Front Cover Illustration by: Fotoluxstudio

*To Chloe, you were the first woman that showed me the possibilities. I would have never known anything different if it was not for you. Go, girl power.*

# CHAPTER ONE

*A*nna got into the car passenger seat. Robert could not look at her. It riddled her with guilt and shame as Robert drove. The house party her friend Julia had arranged was more like a house orgy. Anna could not believe she had just fucked a random gorgeous black man while her husband stood and played with himself. She had to say something before they got home.

"Hun, are you okay?" She asked.

He turned to her with tears rolling down his cheeks.

"I'm such a loser. I feel so empty and useless."

"Oh my God, no. Hun, you're not a loser. I love you. I was just doing those things 'cause I thought that's what you liked. I feel so bad."

The car abruptly pulled over to the side of the road and stopped. Robert turned to his wife.

"Anna, I love you too. I'm not upset at you at all. You did nothing wrong. It's me. I deserve what happened back there. I told you, I feel useless." He patted his eyes with a tissue to remove his tears.

Anna burst into uncontrollable crying as well. It broke her heart in two. Why she allowed herself to do so many wrong things in one night was outside of her own comprehension. Somehow, she had convinced herself that this was the right thing to do. Robert's emotional outburst told a different story.

"Robert, I'm so, so sorry. I promise I will never do that again. I thought it might be fun, but now we're both a mess. I don't know what's gotten into me these days. I swear Julia has some kind of spell over me. Maybe I should stop hanging out with her."

Robert pulled the car forward and then halted as Anna suggested ending her friendship with Julia. He placed his hand on her legs and could feel the skin-tight leather pants.

"No! I don't want you to keep always pleasing me. I'm not saying Julia is the answer, but I have caused all this because I'm so fuddy-duddy in my ways."

It shocked Anna at his lack of support to terminate her association with Julia. Her husband was an emotional mess, and she was not much better herself. It all seemed so confusing and surreal. Almost like the entire night never even happened. Robert carried on driving with an expressionless face, saying nothing else for most of the hour-long drive.

Turning on to their street, Anna felt compelled to keep some form of dialogue going so it didn't get any weirder.

"Hun, I just want you to be happy. I don't want my actions to jeopardize our marriage. You have been so good to me and my children. Say something."

"I don't know what you want me to say, Anna. I feel terrible that I can't satisfy you the way that guy back there did. You should have seen yourself. You looked so happy and excited. I loved seeing you enjoying yourself so much."

Anna could not believe what she was hearing.

"What? You're not upset with me at all? But I feel so dirty. I'm just as upset at myself as you are."

"No, my Goddess, I'm not upset at you at all. I worship you."

It floored Anna. In the two hours from when she first emerged from the basement of Julia's friend's house till now, Robert seemed to have a complete turnaround in his disposition. Perhaps what Julia told her before leaving was true.

"Okay, well, in that case, I seemed to have redeveloped a nasty little habit that needs some nurturing. You go on inside while I have a few puffs." Anna said, trying to recreate the bad girl experience for her husband. And there it was. His pants had a tiny bump as he walked into the garage.

Her head was spinning with confusion. Was he into her cuckolding him or not? Disregarding Julia's advice to with-hold sex, Anna decided she would go inside and see just how much her infidelities impacted her husband's libido while the entire experience was still fresh.

"I'm up here, my Goddess." Came from upstairs as she closed the garage and turned the outside lights off.

Robert had pulled the bed sheets down and lay starfish naked with a full hard-on.

"Oh, my," Anna said in her seductively soft voice. "It seems you have gotten over feeling sorry for yourself there, little boy. It also looks like your little pecker is all excited. Is she excited about fucking me or is she excited about what you saw earlier?"

Robert could barely speak. He placed his arms over his face to hide the excitement and joy, embarrassed. Anna kept her leather pants on and sat by the bedside chair. Looking up, Robert looked distressed and confused.

"Why are you sitting over there? I thought we could... You know." He said.

"Oh, we will. I just want to clear the air. Are you sure you're not upset with me for what I did, cause I feel really guilty." Anna could not help notice his cock lost all its upward momentum in a single sentence. This made no sense. Perhaps he was upset and didn't want her to remind him, she thought to herself.

Wasting no more time, she wiggled out of her leather pants and climbed on the bed. Her hands crept down his chest as she gently placed her tongue into his mouth. The lower her hand went, the more she was sure he would regain his 'manhood'. Finally, she reached his pubic hair and, "what the fuck? You're soft. What did I say? You are still mad at me." Anna said with more guilt filtering back.

"No, I'm not. Let me eat you out. Please!" Robert said with a tone of desperation.

"But, um, I haven't had a shower or anything since, um..."

Before she could finish her sentence, Robert had flipped her on her back, spread her legs wide open, and had his mouth trying to please her with more enthusiasm than she had ever known him to do. He was loving it. Anna found all thoughts evaporate in an instant as he teased her clit over and over and over.

She quickly was done with the surface teasing and

wanted her husband inside her. Pulling his thin gray hair out from in between her legs, she told him to lie down. Thrusting his chest against the bed, she straddled him with both legs and gently guided his cock.

She could feel his cock almost slip in with no effort. It was a noticeable size reduction from her black bull. Perhaps he had stretched her too much.

"Oh, yes." She said to help her husband maintain his woody, but it slowly lost any oomph.

"Tell me how I feel," Robert said as she tried to maintain any sense that he was inside her at all.

"What do you mean?" She asked, unsure what to say.

"Tell me how small I feel. Tell me how good the other guy felt. Tell me I'm a useless fuck. I know it sounds fucked but just do it."

Anna had only seen this side of him recently. Every time, it confused her. The more cruel and insensitive she appeared, the more her husband seemed to like it.

"Okay, you're right. You are fucking useless. I can't feel you at all. I wish I could go back and fuck another one of those guys at the party." She said as she slid back and forth to feel something, anything.

It took the finishing off her last sentence before she could feel her husband rock hard and up to the standards she expected. Now, she could enjoy the feelings.

"Oh yes, yes," she said as the tingling feelings began.

30 seconds later, she could feel her husband had gone limp.

"What's wrong? Did I upset you? I should have said nothing and kept my mouth shut. I'm such a terrible wife."

"No," Robert laughed. "I'm done."

"You're done? Ooookay. I hope it was good for you.

Did you get off?" She dismounted him to find a warm cream rolling down both their legs.

"I love you, Anna, thank you."

"I love you too, Hun. Do we want to talk about this?" Anna asked.

"Nope. I'm good and exhausted. I'm going to sleep. Good night." He said as he leaned over to turn his side-light off.

Anna sat in disbelief. The entire evening was righteously fucked. It seemed like he still wanted her to be a bad girl, but...

They needed to have a serious talk in the morning to clear the air and get things straight before she was going to take any further action in any direction.

# CHAPTER TWO

*It* was after two in the afternoon when Anna opened her eyes. She lay in the empty bed, her head swimming with flashes of the previous night skirting through her thoughts. It felt like a horror and a fantasy movie in one sitting. Did it even happen, or was she dreaming?

The leather pants lying on the floor confirmed it was all real. Her instinct was to go to damage control mode and try to forget any of it happened. Just go back to being the good little housewife she had forced herself to be for the last 10 years.

She then remembered how things ended. Robert liked the whole thing. He blew his load in record time and asked her to tell him he was insufficient as a sex partner. It seemed like a weather channel forecast of up and down. Getting up and putting on some track pants, she went downstairs determined to keep the facade of being a bad girl up based on her husband's reactions.

"Morning" Robert greeted her as she entered the kitchen.

He had resumed his cagy body language and avoidance of any direct eye contact with his wife. Anna felt like she was on an emotional roller coaster ride. Was she to forget? Not forget and carry on as his Hotwife? Be cruel? Beg for forgiveness? This was all getting to be too much.

She poured herself a coffee and asked where the kids were.

"Both are still sleeping in their rooms."

"At 2:17 pm?" She asked

"Ya, you know teens." Robert had nothing else to add.

"Well, good morning," she kissed him on the cheek." I'm going to call Julia and see what she's up to."

"Oh hun, please don't. I don't like you hanging out with her." He said.

Anna took this as an indication that the previous night's frolic was to be forever forgotten.

"I understand, at least let me call her to let her know we got home okay. I know she was very concerned about both of us from, ya know, last night."

"Fine." He said in a gruff.

Anna took her coffee out to the backyard patio to ensure the call to Julia kept a degree of privacy as they spoke.

"Good afternoon Miss Anna," Julia answered the phone exuding a tone of energy and excitement to hear how things went.

"Hello, Julia. Listen, we need to talk."

"Say no more. You got the little bobbies off last night, didn't you?" Julia asked.

"Well, sort of. But I'm not calling to discuss our sex life. Robert and I have been talking and I think this whole cuckold fantasy world thing is just not for us."

There was a prolonged pause before Julia responded.

"Anna, I told you last night. Let me guess. You both got home. He could barely keep his dick in his pants. I guarantee you fucked as you've never fucked before. He loved the idea of seeing you with Brad. And now, today, he has gone back to being his dickish self. How close am I?"

Anna could not believe how accurate Julia's synopsis was. It was like the woman was right there with them.

"How did you know all this?" Anna asked.

"My love, it's a classic case of cuckold angst. It is both your best friend and your worst enemy."

"I'm not sure I understand. All I know is I feel disgusted at myself, my husband seems to be an emotional mess and something tells me, this kind of lifestyle is just not right for us. I mean, yes, I had fun, and it was," Anna hesitated, looking for the appropriate words. "Interesting. But I think it would be best if our paths part ways."

Julia did not want to pressure Anna, nor was she looking to help to destroy a marriage.

"Miss Anna, stop. I completely understand how and why your feeling this way, but you must stop. Let's get together so we can talk about this."

"Julia, I don't know if that's such a good idea. Robert has already expressed he'd prefer we, um, ya know."

"Ok, that makes it official. We need to talk, Anna. Please. Just give me one hour of your time. If what I have to say makes little sense, I will leave you and your little bobbies alone. The cafe by your hospital. 4 pm. I'll see you there my love." Julia intentionally ended the call before giving Anna a chance to decline.

Anna returned inside the house and announced to Robert she was going out.

"What? To see that Julia witch?" He asked.

"Well, yes. I have this leftover pack of cigarettes I'm going to give her and I just wanted to end the friendship face to face." Anna was scrambling to think of any excuse she could offer that would make any sense to her husband.

"Just throw them out, damnit. She has fucked both our lives up. I want to forget last night and this last week as quickly as possible. I mean, look at me, Anna. I'm a fucking mess."

Robert started to tear up as he spoke. His hands were shaking and his eyes continued to avoid contact with Anna, despite the dialogue. Anna felt like she had just been punched in the stomach. Watching her husband continuously fall apart was not her plan. She was committed to getting back to their normal married life as soon as possible.

"Ok, Hun. I'll just be a couple of hours, and then we can put this all behind us. Okay?" She said in a comforting voice, even with her own emotional upheaval.

After a quick shower and change of clothes, Anna got into her car, sending a quick text to Julia.

"LEAVING NOW."

She then put her car in motion and decided to have one last cigarette on the drive, before she closed this brief episode of her life for good.

# CHAPTER THREE

*W*aiting for her at the cafe entrance, Julia ordered them both large cafe lattes and found them a table out on the patio. Anna arrived looking both emotionally and physically exhausted.

"Hello, my love. You look like you've had a very rough start to your day."

"Hi, Julia. Ya, I'm spent. This little 'thing' was fun, but it can't be healthy. Here, by the way." Anna withdrew the half-consumed package of cigarettes and gave them to Julia.

"What's this for?" Julia raising one eyebrow.

"Doing that kind of thing is from my past. I gave up my party day life when Robert came into my life. I don't want to go back."

Julia placed them on the table and withdrew any sense of consolation to her friend.

"Oh, I see. So you think about what you did last night.

What you and little bobbies openly told each other the day before. It was all just fun and games, is that right?" Julia asked.

"It had to be. We both feel horrible now. I'm sure we would both rather forget the last 72 hours and just go back to our normal life." Anna picked up her latte to take a sip of the steaming hot beverage.

Julia followed, taking a sip of her beverage and intentionally let the silence become uncomfortable. If Anna did not know any better, it looked like Julia was angry or disappointed.

"What's wrong, Julia? You look like you don't get it."

"Oh, I get it. The problem is you, my love, still have a lot of learning to do."

Anna shook her head.

"No. No, I do not. I'm done, Julia. This may be a lifestyle that works for you and your husband, but it's just too weird for us."

Julia moved her hand on top of Anna's comfortingly.

"Miss Anna, you've missed the point. You don't have a choice."

Anna pulled her hand away, not expecting the forceful response.

"Excuse me? Who do you think you are? You can't force Robert and I. I think I should go, now."

"No, no, no, Anna, listen to what I'm saying here. I don't mean I'm about to force you to do anything you don't want. Of course not. What I'm saying is you and little bobbies don't have a choice moving forward as a cuckold couple. I've seen this happen, I don't know how many times. Cuckolding is in your blood. Both of you. It's what you both really want. What's happening to both of you now is what I like to call the adjustment period."

"No, Julia. We were just fine before you came into my life. Cuckolding is fucked. Yes, it was extremely fun and exciting for me, but it's not worth the emotional damage. We're done."

"Miss Anna, NO YOU'RE NOT. Stop for a minute. Let's look at the whole thing objectively here. Before you met me, were you truly happy with your marriage? Did you feel appreciated? Were you 'satisfied'? Did little bobbies get excited as much, or even at all?"

"Well..." Anna tried to defend herself.

"Well, what? You know what happened was amazing for you. And let's not even talk about little bobbies. He was adoring, attentive, and, well, I guess it didn't turn him on? I guess that's the problem?"

"Oh no, it turned us both on. But it was just a phase. Just a little kink to add spark to our lives." Anna was not even convincing herself with her lack of conviction.

"Right. 'Just a phase'? Girlfriend, think damnit. Think! I watched you get fucked silly with that magnificent black specimen, Brad. You can tell me whatever you want, but I know you were in heaven. Something I didn't tell you about your little bobbies was he was there almost the entire time. Did he stop you? Did he yell at you? Was he so turned on that he didn't care that I was in the room, he had to beat off? Really, Anna? Really?"

"What are you saying, Julia?"

"What I'm saying is you are a true cuckoldress. A Goddess to your little bobbies. You loved it. It came as natural to you as breathing. Your bobbies also loved it. He didn't just love it, he asked you to do it. And you don't realize it yet, but he will want you to do it again and again and again. Now that he has seen it. Now that he has felt how wonderful it is to be cuckolded, he cannot be truly happy any other way. Frankly, neither will you. This is in your blood. The fact that you are both this way, you do not have a choice. It is something that now has to happen. It is part of who you both are as a couple."

Anna was speechless. She wanted to object vehemently but found it impossible to say anything. Julia continued.

"Miss Anna, I can see by your face, you want to leave this lifestyle. Really, I can see that. But I can also see that deep down inside yourself, you know what I've said is 100% the undeniable truth. You want to fight it in your head. Your heart always wins, and you and I both know your heart wants more. Stop fighting the inevitable and let's deal with the real elephant in the room. What do you do now?"

Anna tried to fight the urge to smile, but she knew Julia was completely on point. There was nothing she could do but accept the truth.

"Can I have my cigarettes back?" Anna said with a sheepish acknowledgment that Julia was right.

The two women talked well past the dinner hour, scheming every action Anna should take to avoid constant reoccurrences of the day's trauma. Julia provided Anna with a shopping list of items she would need to pick up before she arrived home. Most of the items seemed alien except for the pantyhose.

"Why do you want me to pick up pantyhose?" Anna asked.

"Oh my love, you need to speed up your learning curve, my dear. I asked you what things turned little bobbies on the absolute most. You said pantyhose fetish was his big thing. Now you will have his kryptonite."

"Uh?" Anna felt stupid but needed Julia to give her step-by-step instructions for the when and how.

Anna left shortly after and headed directly to the east side of town, where she knew of only one adult toy store. Fortunately, it was also close to a variety store where she resolved to pick up a carton of cigarettes. 'Go big, or go home' was her thoughts as she pulled into the driveway of her home.

# CHAPTER FOUR

*A*nna could tell as she entered the house that Robert had not whacked off. Her late arrival normally resulted in a series of complaints, particularly given who she just finished seeing. Tonight, Robert seemed rather agreeable, which would work perfectly for the plan Julia and her had discussed.

"Hey, Rob. Sorry, I'm later than expected. I had to run by a store and pick up a few things on the way home."

"No worries, my love." He responded in a very submissive tone.

Anna could smell the excessive cigarette smoke in her hair and clothes. She was sure Rob would complain. He remained silent.

"I'm going upstairs to change into something a little more comfortable, do you mind?" She asked, not expecting the response given.

"Of course, my dear. Can I serve our dinners, or did you want me to wait?"

Anna could see that Julia was right on the money. Give a cuck enough time away from orgasm and he wants to relive the entire experience over and over and over again. She could not believe she had missed this side of her husband for so many years.

"Yes, wait, please. We need to talk. I'll explain when I come back down. Are the kids home?"

"No. One's out at a friends, and the other is at work."

Anna quickly ran upstairs with her shopping bags, unpacked the most important item, familiarizing herself with how it worked. She removed her panties and put on the sheer hose, one of Rob's dress shirts, and covered the little outfit with a terry-cloth robe to offer some concealment.

When she entered the kitchen, Rob was standing at the stove making last preparations to serve the dinner once they finished talking. He had yet to notice Anna's 'more comfortable' selection of clothing.

"Hun, don't ask, just trust me," Anna said to his back.

"What?" He turned around with a confused look on his face.

"Drop your pants. Right now. Go on, drop them."

Rob quickly eyed her up and down. He immediately saw that she had on the tan hosiery that he so loved to see her in. Without questioning or hesitation, he obliged, undoing his belt and dropping his pants. Anna smiled and pulled her right hand around from behind her back.

"What the hell is that?" Rob looked at a cylindrical object that vaguely resembled the shape of a dick.

"I'd rather show you than tell you, my love. Here, let's try this on for a second."

Anna gently applied a small amount of lubrication from the small tube that came with the device. She then slowly slid Robert's cock into the unit. With each motion, she tried to minimize any form of stimulation. She also knew she had to hurry. If he became fully erect before it was on, it would be next to impossible to fit. Once the unit was on firmly, she swung the hanging section of the device. It went around the circumference of his bag sack and reattached itself back at the top of the unit.

Robert looked at her, unsure what the hell she was doing.

"Hun, I'm not sure what the heck this thing is, but if it's supposed to get me off, I'm not feeling it."

Anna looked up to him with a devilish smile and then reached into her robe pocket. She removed a micro padlock that was not one of those pretend ones you see on a suitcase. It looked more substantive.

"I know my little robbies." She said as the lock worked its way through the latching mechanism and clicked shut.

"Hey. What the fuck? What the hell is this?" Rob asked, but quickly figuring out the essence of its intended use.

Anna opened her robe for a sneak peek and told him to have a seat. Despite the visual appeal of seeing his wife in his favorite hosiery, he was still in shock. His cock showed no sign of appreciation.

"So I have talked to Julia, and she has helped me see who we really are as a married couple. She has set me back on the right path. I now understand you so much better.

You are a true cuckold, my princess. I know it from the bottom of my heart, and let's be honest here, so do you."

Rob's face turned red with excitement and embarrassment. She untied the robe and let it fall to the ground.

"Likewise, look at me. LOOK AT ME DAMNIT! I'm hot as fuck. I know it and so do you."

Rob nodded in agreement but remained silent.

"I deserve to be fucked hard. Real hard. Real often. Don't I? I SAID DON'T I?"

He silently agreed again.

"And you absolutely love me being a bad little girl," Anna said as she pointed to his caged cock. It was screaming for space as the constraints of the cage would only let him get hard to a point, then pain and discomfort kicked in.

"Y Y Y Yes my Goddess."

There it was. That rush of complete power and control. Anna hated being mean to her husband. She loved him so much and did not want to hurt him. It was Julia, who made her finally realize her actions were not mean, or bad, or evil. They were the kindest, caring, and loving things she could do for this man. She could see he loved this. She loved this. They both loved this. Why was she fighting herself?

"That's right. I am your Goddess. I'm not your wife, your 'Hun', or Anna. And you, my little bobbies, you are my sweet and sexy little princess. You are, you know. You're my little princess. You like that, don't you? Oh look, there he grows again." Anna giggled and pointed at his cock. Rob was humiliated and loving every single second of it.

"You want this, don't you, my sweet little princess?"

"Y Y Yes, my Goddess." He stuttered in uncontrollable excitement.

"That's what I thought. So Julia has told me about how you work. Once you blow your load, you go back to being an old fart of a dick. I feel guilty and you feel like a loser. It's crazy when you think about it."

"I I I c c c can't help it."

"Shut the fuck up! This is what we're going to do. Tonight, you're going to keep this cage on. Tomorrow, I want you to go to work with this cage on. And then tomorrow night, maybe. Just maybe, we can talk again."

He looked like he had just drunk the elixir of life, joy, and happiness.

"Yes, m m my Goddess."

"Good. Now put your mouth to good use. I have these hose on and I need to feel you appreciate all the hard work I've done to look sexy for you."

Anna took his hand, led him to the couch, and pushed him to the floor.

"Get on your knees, my princess."

She lay back, spread her legs, and the princess began licking like his tongue could cut a hole in her pantyhose with the friction.

"That's a good little princess." Her eyes rolled to the back of her head as the sensations intensified and took over her entire body.

Anna loved this. The memories of Brad pounding her slipped in and out of her mind while she looked down to her husband's head moving up and down like a frenzied little girl. She could feel all the energy centers of her body activated all at once. All her muscles began contracting all at once. Her core started vibrating.

"Oh, Yessssss." She breathed.

Every part of her body felt a release. All the guilt. All the emotionalism from the previous day. Everything just felt as it should be. She looked into her husband's face. He was begging for reciprocation.

"No, my little princess. You're done. Come on. Let's have dinner and go to bed."

Despite the anguish and sexual frustration, Rob seemed to accept her demands with no rebuttal. Anna knew Julia had something. She was right for a second time. Tomorrow a more detailed plan needed to be discussed with Miss Julia.

# CHAPTER FIVE

*A*nna woke up to an empty house. Both kids were at school and her husband had left for work. She sent Julia a text suggesting they meet up for a mid-day coffee at their usual place. Julia sent a three-word response, "see you there". Anna pulled out some frozen meat from the freezer to thaw for the dinner, went to collect the mail, and started a load of laundry, before heading out.

For the first time in their friendship, Julia was not there ahead of Anna. She struggled to remember how Julia took her coffee as she placed their orders. The sun was hot, Anna thought to herself as she grabbed a table with an umbrella on the patio. Like clockwork, Julia arrived just as she sat down and lit a cigarette.

"Hello, my love," Anna said with Julia's style and tone.

"Well, hello Miss Anna. You look a lot better today. I take it things went well last night?"

"Julia, you should have seen him. He was like a lost puppy dog. I admit it. You were right. He is a cuckold."

Julia nodded in praise and confirmation.

"The question is my dear, how did you feel? Do you feel guilty now about your actions a couple of nights ago? Do you feel guilty about regaining control over the relationship?"

"I don't know. I mean, I just remembered on the drive over here that he's still got that cock cage locked on. It was fun last night, but now that the moment is over..." Anna responded.

Julia placed her coffee on the table and leaned across the table to hug Anna.

"Miss Anna, I'm so proud of you. You are becoming my best protege ever."

Anna looked at Julia with a puzzled look.

"'Protege'? What do you mean? I hope you're not suggesting I'm a pet project for you or something." She said with annoying concern.

Julia took a large drag off her cigarette, giving her a moment to think how she would deliver the news.

"Miss Anna, I have been married for over 15 years. Fluffy and I have been cuckolding almost the entire time. Samantha, a woman I met shortly after we married, introduced me to cuckolding. She helped guide me, encourage me, coach me. I have many friends and none are as happy in their marriage as I have been. I owe it to Sam. Since then, whenever I see a chance to bring another couple into the light, I do what I can."

Pursing her lips, Anna asked, "So, how many women have you helped?"

"Oh, I don't know. I don't keep count, but at least a

dozen. Probably more. The party I invited you to was one of those couples."

Anna was unsure how she felt. Was this woman across from her a homewrecker? Was she an angel? So far, Julia had turned her relationship with Robert upside down. Was it for the better? Anna instinctively wanted to pump the breaks.

Julia could see the pensive look on Anna's face. She put her hand out to touch her arm.

"Anna, it's okay. Trust me. I know what I'm doing. I'm not helping you for kicks. I really care about you and little bobbies."

Anna smiled and stopped her mid-sentence.

"Nope. He is no longer little bobbies. I gave him the name princess."

"Oh, I love that! It's so cute and humiliating. That must drive him crazy. You see, this is what I'm talking about. Anna, this entire lifestyle comes naturally to you. It's who you are. And for the princess to willingly follow, it's who he is. I'm telling you, I know our kind. I could tell the first day we met, you belonged in our Goddess fold."

Leaning back to stretch, Anna felt a deep sense of comfort. It was such a fucked situation that was wrong on so many levels. Yet, to her, it just felt so right, so good, so.... She would continue Julia's path, at least for a little while longer.

"Well, thanks, Julia. So, anyway, I told my little princess that he was to keep the cage on until this evening when we would talk again. But now, I have no idea what to do or where to take things."

Julia stood up. Outed her cigarette and put her sunglasses on before turning to Anna.

"Come on. Let's go. I have somewhere you must go. Do you have your purse and ID?"

Anna was curious and confused.

"But, I wanted to talk. And yes, I have my purse. Where are you taking me, Julia?"

"Miss Anna, how many times do I have to tell you. Just trust me. This time next year, your life will look so much different and better. Come on, we don't have a lot of time. What time do you work?"

"Ugh, I'm on afternoons again."

The two women traveled several blocks. Anna could not help notice the dozens of men that seemed to admire Julia as they walked. Julia was no more attractive than herself but she was like a guy magnet. Perhaps it was her choice of short shorts and a tight-fitting top? They finally stopped in front of an enormous building in the financial district.

"Ok, Julia. I give up. Where the fuck are you taking me?"

"We're here, Miss Anna." Julia pointed to the bank in front of them.

"A bank? You need to do some banking and you brought me along for the ride?"

Julia giggled at Anna's innocence.

"No, my love. You are going to open an account."

"But why? Robert and I already do our banking elsewhere."

"Exactly. I'll explain when we get inside." Julia grabbed Anna's hand in a motherly fashion and pulled her into the building.

Two hours later, both women exited the building laughing at the branch manager's uncomfortable need to remain seated in his office cubicle as Julia flirted hardcore.

"Julia, I hope I'm doing the right thing here," Anna said.

"We're not done. You need to do everything else I said as well. Remember, when little princess gets home, wind him up just a little. He's got the cage on so it'll hurt."

Again, both women began laughing as they headed back to their cars.

# CHAPTER SIX

*a*nna had just enough time to print out the letter and apply some make-up when her husband slammed the door shut.

"Hello. Anna?" He shouted at the front door.

"I'm upstairs. I'll be down in a few." She responded.

She slipped on some hosiery and into her tightest fitting jeans. She left the bathroom, knowing he'd pick up on her attire instantly, without looking inappropriate for the kids if they came home unexpectedly.

"Hun, I need this thing off, like now!" Robert said as she walked into the room.

She smiled but remained silent. She bent over to light a candle, revealing the hosiery that was underneath from behind. His eyes darted to her feet to confirm she was indeed wearing them. An instant smile came over his face, followed by a look of confusion.

"How come you're not in your work scrubs? I thought

you were on afternoons this week." He paused. "Ah, so I guess if you're not going in until the night shift we have some evening playtime. I see." He was bordering on salivation.

"Oh, no. I'm going to work. Actually, I have to leave earlier than normal." Anna intentionally left her words ambiguous.

"But? Why the?" He said with growing confusion.

"Let me stop you right there, my little princess. I have had some more time to think this through. We are not playing anymore. This is the real deal. We both love it, so why do we both keep fighting this?" Again, she wanted to leave as much blank information so he would enter his cucky headspace without delay.

"Um, okay? But I still need this cage off. It's driving me nuts. And I still don't understand why your not in your work uniform." He said.

"I'm going to work to give them this." Anna handed her husband the page she had just finished printing out.

He put his reading glasses on, placing one hand on his forehead as he read. His face scrunched up and swung from side to side. He put the paper on the table and looked up in disbelief.

"So you're quitting? You've decided to quit a job that you've been at for over a decade? Why? How come we never talked about this? I mean, we'll be okay on just my income, but this is a big deal, Anna. What the fuck?"

Anna moved the table just enough to stand in front of him. She lifted one leg and placed her foot into her husband's crotch. Her stocking-clad foot was right in his face as she eased up and down his cock.

"Listen, my baby little princess. For you, I am no

longer Anna. I am to be called 'Goddess' at all times, under all circumstances."

She could feel his cock struggling to escape its confinement. Discomfort and confusion on his face.

"But, but..."

"Shut the fuck up. I deserve more than that shit job. I've been working my beautiful ass off for years, for what? To give you my money so you can go buy that new set of golf clubs? So you can buy your executive lunches at expensive restaurants? So you can have subscriptions to all those specialty sports networks? Fuck that shit. It's over. I mean, it's really fucking over. This is not a game anymore, my little princess. I don't want to go back to the boring life we had. Do you understand?"

He was there. He was now in the headspace she needed him to be in. He acknowledged his understanding with a nod.

"Good. Here's how things are going to go. I am now in charge of everything. You are my little princess. If you treat me well. I mean, VERY WELL..." she let out a subtle sigh of contempt, then continued. "I will reward you if you know what I mean." She moved her foot up and down his shaft, feeling his cock screaming for space.

"I am to be the center of your universe. Your life is about making me happy. Isn't that what all good little princesses do for the Goddesses?"

"Y Y Yes, my Goddess." He responded without contest.

"Very good. So you now understand why I'm quitting. I need to have more time to take care of my needs. I have so many needs, my little princess. They have all gone so long without being satisfied."

"Y Y Yes d d dear... I mean G G Goddess."

Anna could feel herself getting wet. The power felt so good. The more she took from her husband, the better it felt. It tempted her to make him cry when she remembered Sophia's cautionary words about taking baby steps. Too much, too quick, could backfire. She needed to bring her husband into the life, one piece at a time. Eventually, it would all come naturally to both of them.

"Excellent. I'm glad you agree that this is best for both of us. You think this is what's best for you, don't you, my cute little princess? You want me to keep being happy. And..." She lifted her hand to her face, intentionally laughing in a sexually humiliating way. "And you want to be my princess. You yearn for it. You desperately feel the need and want of being your Goddess's little princess, don't you?"

His face went a deep red. Looking to the ground, he shook his head.

"Good little princess. I love when we can agree with such sweetness and love."

"But Anna, this is your jo.."

Anna did not know where it came from, but the look of rage jumped into her eyes.

"SHUT THE FUCK UP!" Thrusting her foot into his crotch to cause pain.

"My little princess needs to be a good little girl. If you have any hope of ever seeing your cage removed, you need to listen. You like me this way. You want this just as much as I do. I've got to be the strong one in this relationship and make it happen cause your too much a baby. Yup, a baby little princess. Am I right?"

He had passed the point of no return. His mind was

screaming fight, fight, fight. His heart and soul wanted nothing more than to thank Anna. His heart had won the battle.

"Yes, my Goddess. I am yours. I beg of you. Please do what's right for us. I beg you."

Anna moved her foot and passed him another form.

"Here. You need to take this to your Human Resources department at work tomorrow."

"What is it?" He asked.

"It's a direct deposit request. I want all future money you make deposited into this account. Don't worry, I'll make sure I give you an allowance." Snickering as she left the room to go to the kitchen and get a scrap piece of paper and pen. Returning, she sat down, crossed her legs, being sure to have her stocking feet in full view.

"Here is a list of things I need you to do while I go drop off my resignation."

On the page:

Fluff my laundry in the dryer, fold and put away - panties go in top right drawer

Take load in washer and put into dryer - when done, same as above

Prepare dinner - ground beef is in fridge - spaghetti sauce in the cupboard

Clean downstairs toilet and sink

It was at this point Robert, Rob, Bob, bobbies; they all died. He was a little princess. The internal fight felt like it was over. It scared him, but he felt happier than he had in years. His wife knew him better than he knew himself. She was truly his Goddess.

"Yes, my Goddess. If you need anything else, please

text or call me. I just want to thank you and tell you I love you and that you're the best."

Anna turned, raised her hand, and isolated her middle finger as she went to leave. The door closed with a thud. The little princess was sure he could feel dampness in his pants.

Ten minutes later, his phone rang with Anna's caller id showing.

"Yes, my Goddess."

"One other thing. Forget dropping the form to HR tomorrow. I want you to call in sick. You can take care of that the next day."

"W W Why do you w w want me to call in s s sick?"

"Oh, my little princess, you're taking me shopping. I have so many new things I want. I need to look good if I want to attract real men into our life." She whispered as she abruptly hung the phone up, leaving him no chance to respond.

## CHAPTER SEVEN

A strong and aromatic smell of coffee filtered into the bedroom as the early morning light hinted another sunny and warm day was in store. Anna glanced at the night table clock. This was the earliest she had woken all week. Stretching as she stood up, she remembered this was not a weekend. Her mind kept going back and forth from her current reality to the one she's known for years. It was scary to feel she was traveling in uncharted territory.

This was her alternative world. Unexpectedly, her mind panicked. She had tendered her resignation last night, and she had all but forced Robert to call in sick. Her world was changing way too fast and in such magnitude. This was huge. Some of this stuff she just couldn't undo. Was she taking things too far? 'What have I done?' She asked herself. Perhaps it was not too late to send her husband to work. Maybe he did not call his boss yet. Maybe she could get her job back. She threw on some shorts and a T-shirt and leaped down the stairs to catch her husband before he made the call.

"Good morning, my Goddess," Robert said

"Good morning, Hun. Did you call your work yet?"

"Why yes, my Goddess. I am completely yours for the day. I've made you a fresh pot of coffee and I set up the deck outside with an ashtray so you can have a cigarette with it."

"So it's too late to call back and say your coming in?" Anna asked.

Her husband looked confused and concerned.

"Um, kinda. I'm not sure what excuse I could give them at this point. Why? I thought you wanted me to take you for an all-day shopping experience." His actions and body language screaming to be as attentive to her needs as possible.

She wanted to reverse everything. She wanted to go back to the old way they were. It was just all too bizarre. It seemed like the right thing to do last night, but now it felt like everything was wrong. This was too much change. She was having a panic attack.

"My Goddess, you look upset. Have I done something wrong?"

Anna barely heard anything he was saying. Her mind was racing in fear. It was all a mistake. She had changed things she could not change back. She needed time to think.

"Huh? Oh, sorry, Robert. I'm really distracted. I need some time to think and wake up." She said as she poured her coffee and went out to the deck and naturally went to light a cigarette.

She turned around just before closing the sliding door and asked if Robert could pass her phone. She needed Julia to help her make sense of what she was feeling.

"Hello, my love. You're up bright and early. It's only 8:37 am."

"Hey, Julia. Listen, we need to talk. I'm rethinking this whole lifestyle thing. I think I've made a huge mistake. I'm freaking out here." Anna said.

"Miss Anna, get a hold of yourself. Stop thinking for just one second."

"But I just quit my job and I told Robert to..."

"STOP. Listen to yourself. You're panicking for no reason. Yes, you have made some monumental changes in a brief period. And yes, some things you can't undo. Where's your little princess right now? Is he in front of you?"

"No. He's inside in the kitchen. I'm out on the deck having a smoke."

"Good girl. So take a moment. Look at your little princess. Is he upset? Does he look stressed out? Is he angry with you? Before you answer, I can tell you, he's probably almost dancing around the kitchen with glee, like a little girl. Am I right?"

Anna paused the conversation and looked inside through the glass. Sure enough, Robert was standing at the sink, wiping down the counters. He had a bounce to his step, and he looked at peace. She turned back to the phone.

"Okay, I see what you're saying. What's your point, Julia?"

"My point is you are fighting with yourself, no one else. Even your little princess has stopped fighting. I'm sure the cage has helped with that, but still. The sooner you embrace you are who you are and your husband is who he is, the sooner you'll begin to really grow into being a cuckoldress. We both know it's inevitable. Stop fighting the need to go back to the boring, mundane, and unhappy life that you knew."

"But what if we change our minds after we make all these changes to our marriage? I mean the deeper I go, the more I won't be able to change or erase."

"Anna, please. Look at him. He is wearing a cage. You've already fucked another guy in front of him. You've quit your job and made him give you all his money. And he's thrilled. I'll bet he looks happier than ever." Julia's words provided an immense comfort.

Anna knew what Julia was saying was accurate.

"I don't know. I just feel so guilty and like I'm a bad person for doing all this to him."

"Anna, you are not a bad person and neither is your husband. You love each other deeply. And you both love the cuckold dynamics. So fuck society. You both need this. When you catch yourself thinking your mean or bad to the princess, know that he loves you even more BECAUSE you're being that way."

"Thank you, Julia. Believe it or not, your words are a little comforting, but this is going to take some time to get used to."

Julia giggled.

"Not as much time as you think, my love. So, today. What's the plans you have for the little princess and yourself?"

"Well, I was going to take him to the mall and have him buy me some really sexy outfits that I know other guys will like. I wanted to make sure he knew I was buying them not for him."

"You see. There you go, girl. You're a natural at this. That sounds lovely. Are you going to buy him a little sexy number too?"

"I never thought about it, but I see where you're going and I like it. Tell me more."

The two women talked for almost an hour, while her princess did another load of the household laundry. By the time Anna got off the phone, she was re-centered and back to feeling good about the direction her marriage was going and wanted more. It was now time to see how her little baby princess liked being humiliated.

# CHAPTER EIGHT

The mall was surprisingly busy for mid-week at the lunch hour. The entire morning her little princess was so attentive, he was behaving like he had done something wrong and was trying to make up for it. Anna was seeing the rewards in her husband's disposition since she put the cock cage on. He dropped her off at the front doors, so she could have a smoke while he parked the car and walked the full distance in.

As he approached Anna from the parking lot, several women who looked like they worked in the mall were standing nearby, also attending to their nicotine needs. Anna saw this as a perfect first opportunity.

"Hello, my princess. Thank you so much for being such-a-good-buoy." She said loud enough that the other women turned to see who she was talking to.

It caught her husband off guard. His face went red instantly as he avoided looking at the other women, desperate to go inside and hide. Anna insisted he stay with her while she finished, making sure she spoke loud enough to be overheard. She asked him how his little pee-pee was feeling in a mother to baby voice, causing the other women to snicker at the ludicrousness of their dialogue.

"The first place I need to go is the women's lingerie stores..."

He smiled but remained silent.

"For you," Anna said as she took his hand and rubbed his wedding ring finger as if she had just proposed to him as the bride.

"What do you think, princess? Would you like me to get you some booty shorts or thongs? I'm thinking you'll look so cute in thongs and your cage. Yes. I'm thinking you're a size small?" Anna recognizing that Julia was right. It all came so naturally and felt inexplicably good.

"Anna. I I I mean, my Goddess. Please stop. I I I am very sore down there and and and,"

Julia's words came back to Anna as her husband pleaded she stop the torment. She would dial the humiliation down a notch till she bought him some nice panties and herself several outfits that could only be worn in a sex club because they would be so scandalous. Then she would exercise her dominance just a little more to see how it felt. $1200 later, Anna suggested it was time for her princess to have a treat of his own. He looked unsure if he liked that idea more than just spoiling her exclusively.

"What would my little princess like? I know, maybe I could buy you a nice ice cream cone and we could sit on one of the benches." She did not give him a chance to respond. She decided.

As they sat on the bench, a young man in his mid-20s

grabbed the seat across. He looked like he had recently graduated from college or university and was now looking for part-time work. He was well dressed. His clothes were tailored perfectly to highlight his lean, muscular body underneath without appearing to be too tight. His deeply tanned face made him look like a model. Anna looked at her husband as he seemed hyper-aware of this young man's presence.

She made sure to make eye contact as she licked her cone suggestively. Long, slow licks, followed by full insertion of the cone as deep into her mouth as she could manage. He smiled, his eyes now locked on her and oblivious to her husband sitting beside her. Anna played with the young man, moving the cone in and out of her mouth, letting her tongue appear only to tease. A glance down to his groin revealed he was enjoying this. Turning to her husband, he was catatonic with admiration of his wife. He was not upset, he was loving this. She leaned over to make sure her breasts displayed more welcoming. She was loving the attention in sexual interest this handsome man was giving her. She felt invincible.

"Hi. I'm Anna."

"Hi there, pretty lady. My name's Todd. Watcha doin' here? I assume you're taking gramps here out for his daily exercise?"

She loved this. It was perfect.

"Something like that." She smiled.

"Listen, I got an interview in 5 minutes, but I'd love to get your number. Maybe we can go have a coffee or somethin?"

Anna pulled her purse up and wrote her number on a scrap of paper. Glancing down, her husband could see she gave her real number and signed it 'call me, Anna XO' as she passed to the stranger.

The princess struggled to walk to the car. He was in pain. It was at that moment Anna realized what was really going on. She could do no wrong. Nothing. Nadda. Zip. She was free to flirt. Free to fuck. Free to do nothing but relax and enjoy life. The more selfish and self-centered Anna became, the more admiration and respect her husband offered. Still struggling to comprehend why, she also recognized the darker she went in dominating and controlling her little princess, the happier and more in love they both seemed to be with each other. It made no sense, but she was living exactly what Julia said would happen.

As they got into the car, her husband could no longer contain himself.

"My Goddess, thank you so much for today. I am so lucky to have you. I mean it. I am the luckiest man alive. Thank you for having me."

Anna was pissed at herself. She couldn't believe that three hours earlier, she wanted to undo everything. She made a promise to herself. That will never happen again. This feels too good and feels too right to just throw away.

"You're very welcome, my little princess. You were a very good little princess. I'm excited about seeing you in your new panties, aren't you?"

The harsh reality that he was losing his manhood hit with his wife's words. He hated he was this way. He wanted to be the dude sitting across from them, but he was not. He never was. He loved the way his wife was treating him. It felt so mean and bad and cruel and absolutely wonderful. He loved it and wanted more. So much more.

"Yes, my Goddess. I think they will look wonderful. Thank you so much. You're the best."

No longer caring about the secondhand smoke, she lit a cigarette before they pulled out of the parking lot and headed back home. She blew the smoke in his direction to ensure he was being violated, as she was sure he would appreciate it.

# CHAPTER NINE

The drive was long enough for Anna to realize she wanted more. Once they were both settled in the house, she told her princess she couldn't wait any longer. She was excited to see her little princess all dressed up in his new panties. It filled his face with a glaze of euphoria.

"No, I want you to change right here in front of me. And as a special surprise, I'm going to unlock you for now."

On Julia's advice, Anna had placed the key on a chain around her neck. She unlocked the padlock and slid the cage off, struggling with her husband's semi-erect dick.

"Oh, thank you, my Goddess." He said as he practically ripped his pants to the ground and went to the bag to get the thongs. His hands were shaking with excitement.

"I want to see you in the white ones today," Anna said as he looked unsure which color he should put on.

Anna made him stand in the middle of the hall, while she walked around to inspect how tight they ran up his ass cheeks. The front panel was just big enough to cover up his cock.

"I like this princess. I mean, I REALLY like this little thing on you. It makes you look so cute and girly. I think it suits you perfectly."

He smiled bashfully. She could tell her words were degrading and humiliating to any man, but to her cuckold husband, he would learn to love her more because of them.

"So, I was thinking. I liked that Todd guy we met at the mall. I'd like to fuck him. Yup. I'd like to fuck him real good. Would you like me to fuck him, princess? Did you want to see your Goddess have his dick rammed inside my mouth just like that cone I was eating? Yes? You'd love that. You want that for your Goddess, don't you, my sweet little princess?"

Her husband's cock burst out of the limited thong material and stood at 110 degrees. He was so excited. This was incredible. It seemed Todd aroused Anna, and she also became aroused because her husband was so aroused. The more she expressed the desire, the hotter it made her to see her husband equally enjoying the possibilities. A never-ending circle that seemed to feed itself.

"Well, I gave him my number, but I wasn't smart enough to get his. Maybe he'll call later today, but I don't want to wait. I need to feel a big, hard dick, deep inside me. I need to feel desired, like a sex goddess. I know you can't do that anymore so, what am I to do? What am I to do?" Anna said this with tease written all over it.

"I know! I think you should call Julia. She is such a

good friend to you, my Goddess. I'm sure she knows someone," the princess said voluntarily.

"Good idea, my little princess. I'll do that. In the meantime, let me put your cage back on."

He looked so disappointed but did not want any of it to end.

"There you go. Now keep your new panties on and pull your pants back up before the kids get home from school. I'm going to call Julia."

20 minutes later, Anna emerged from the garage announcing that Julia was so happy about his new panties. Unfortunately, Anna would have to wait until tomorrow for things to happen. Her language was intentionally obtuse, so it left her husband not understanding anything she said beyond sharing the fact that he was now wearing a woman's undergarment.

"I have a unique plan for us tonight that might do," She said with a devious look.

By the time dinner was consumed and the kids were off in their bedrooms, Anna was ready to elaborate enough that her little princess would understand he was her bitch unquestioningly. Anna had already changed into track pants and a sweatshirt.

"Let's go upstairs and play."

"Yes, my Goddess. Can you take this cage off?" He asked like a child to his mommy.

Anna shook her head and laughed.

"Oh, my sweet little princess. You just don't get it. I will take it off." She left him hanging with the assumption it would be once they were in bed.

They got to the bedroom door when Anna asked him to go back down and grab the bag of goodies she had purchased a few days back. He returned slightly out of breath, with her lying naked on her back.

"Here you go, my Goddess. Can you take this off me now?"

She abruptly sat up and gave the illusion she was considering it.

"Um, let me see. NOPE! Are you fucking serious? Do you think I'm going to please you when my own needs have gone unmet for so many fucking years? Not a fucking chance."

"But but but you said downstairs that you'd take it off and..."

"I did indeed. But I didn't say when did I?"

"Anna, that's not fair. That's..."

"What did you just call me? Really? For that, I'm keeping it on even longer than I originally planned. I own you, bitch! We both love it like this, so get over your selfish needs and take my new toys out of the bag. Time to please your Goddess." Anna tried delivering this in the sternest voice she could without raising the volume so loud the kids could hear.

Enclosed were a vibrator, a facemask dildo, handcuffs, and several bottles of personal lubricant. The princess looked at the dildo, with no idea how it was to be used. Anna felt bad, degrading her husband so much, but pushed on.

"It straps around your face, silly girl. You're going to get me wet with the vibrator and your mouth. Then you're going to fuck me with your face. Isn't that so cute?" She couldn't believe where this darkness was coming from, but it felt easy.

Her husband didn't look pleased or aroused. This was a problem she needed to end.

"By the way, you're calling in sick tomorrow as well. We're going over to Julia's for lunch and you're going to sit a watch me. I hope you don't mind. Actually, I'm lying. I don't give a fuck what you think." Anna knew this was only a partial lie.

The princess went straight to task. His mouth gasping for air as he hurried his mouth. Anna sank her head into the pillow, her body feeling enveloped with tingles everywhere. She had never seen her husband so concerned about her satisfaction. His focus was solely on her pleasure. The vibrator moved up and down her clit with just the right amount of pressure and motion.

"Okay, stop licking and start fucking me with your face, cause that thing down there you call a cock, is fucking useless to me." She commanded.

His humiliation became irrelevant. All he wanted was to see his wife's face contort to a place of utter joy. The straps snapped as he placed the unit around his head. He looked like Pinocchio, the pretend dick looking more like a nose as it stalled his face. Anna looked down at him, thinking he looked like a complete fucking idiot. She was quickly learning to love the humiliation.

The dildo straps slapped against her thighs, causing significant discomfort.

"Ok, ok, stop. Take it off and give it to me."

Anna grabbed the vibrator and snapped the dildo off its mount. She pushed her princess off the bed and began using both toys on herself. The frustration of having to please herself killed the mood in seconds.

"Fuck it! You're a good little princess, but you're

fucking useless to me. Let me take the cage off and at least give you something to think about."

He approached the bed with an almost impossible erection. It was too rigid to attempt removal.

"Please, my Goddess. I beg of you. Please get it off."

Anna remembered Julia's cautionary words. "Once he gets off, he goes back to the dick smack man you've always known. Be very careful when and where you let this happen."

Anna patted the bed, suggesting he sit. She turned to the bag that contained her toys and withdrew one of the bottles of lubricant. She turned the bottle upside down and squeezed enough for the bottle to make a farting sound.

She could feel the cage was unwilling to move in any direction as she slowly applied a liberal amount directly on his head. He sat, looking incapable of anything, including speech. She began to repeatedly rub in a circular motion the head of his cock through the cage with her thumb. Anna leaned into his ear and softly spoke.

"You like how this feels my little tender princess. Relax and enjoy it. Think about how much fun we are going to have tomorrow. Look at your poor little cock wanting out of his cage. Poor little baby. You look pathetic. It feels good to be like this, doesn't it?"

Her thumb moving faster and faster in circles, only making partial contact with random exposed parts of his helmet. It looked uncomfortable, and yet there it was. Tiny drops of a creamy white solution slowly bubbling out his spout. His need to explode was constrained by the pain the cage provided.

Abruptly, Anna stopped as the creamy solution

increased in volume. She got up, went to the bathroom, came back with a towel, throwing at him as his body convulsed with sexual energy.

"Here, clean that shit up, princess. Be a doll and have my coffee ready when I wake tomorrow morning. K. Thanks, baby. Good night." Anna turned the light off on her side of the bed and rolled to have her back facing her husband.

As she put her head on the pillow, she felt bad again. It came out of nowhere. She did not know she could be so mean and cruel to the man she loved and cared for so much. She was a terrible human being. She was convinced this was a mistake. Just at that moment, his warm body came next to her. His arm wrapped around her petite figure.

"Thank you so much, my Goddess. I am so lucky to have you. I love you so much. Good night." Came from her husband.

Anna closed her eyes, feeling an electric shock of excitement through her body. She did own him. She was his God. She was wet again.

## CHAPTER TEN

*S*teaming hot with the blazing sun. Not a cloud in the sky. Anna's constant Yo-Yo concerns about doing the right thing seemed to evaporate with the heat. Her husband loved the new Miss Anna. She could no longer pretend to herself. She loved the new her too. This was who she really wanted to be, but was always afraid of what others would think. Not today.

She made sure she was in top form for their little 'get-together'. Black dress shorts with some black nylons underneath. Red pump shoes and her hair pulled back in a ponytail. Her husband was gaga the entire drive. He did not know what Julia had in mind.

"Wow, look at her house. I didn't realize they were that loaded." Anna said as they pulled into the driveway.

Julia answered the door, dressed in almost the same outfit, minus the red shoes and top. The two women gave each other a hug and kiss before Julia extended her hand to the princess. Like a queen, he was not worthy of a full embrace.

"Come in, come in, my loves. The boys are waiting in the games room." Julia said.

"W W Where is is is your husband?" Princess asked.

The two women looked at each other and giggled. Princess sensed they had discussed the day in greater detail than they made him privy to.

"Oh, little princess. I have sent fluffy to his office for the day. I want this to be a very special day for you. A day that you will always cherish. You need to experience this all by your lonesome self. Is that going to be okay for the little baby princess?" Julia spoke in a condescending child-like voice.

"Y Y Y Yes madam," Princess replied as he bowed his head in shame for being reduced to such a zero as an adult.

"That's a good little princess. Now take off your trousers. That's what old people call their pants, isn't it? I want to see the pretty little cage that Miss Anna has been so kind to get for you," Julia continued to belittle him without reserve.

Princess removed his pants and stood in the hallway. The only adult undressed. Julia pointed to his cock and laughed hysterically with Anna.

"You see what I've had to live with for so many years?" Anna said.

"Oh Miss Anna, we are going to fix this in a hurry. Yes, I see. You need and deserve to have more," Julia snickered as she continued. "I mean a lot more. He's pathetic. I mean, look at him. Poor little princess."

As both women continued the banter back and forth, the princess's cock expanded to the limit the cage would permit. Both women could see he loved the humiliation, which only fueled the condemning.

They moved through the house to a set of stairs leading down. The smell of rich masculine cologne strengthened as they descended. The absence of any daylight made the passage of time and day irrelevant. The room was lit with dozens of candles and nothing else.

"Oh, Julia, this is lovely," Anna said as she looked around the room to four gorgeous men in their early 30s. Two black and two caucasian.

All four men wore dress pants and dress shirts with all buttons open, fully exposing their muscular physiques. They put most men to shame any day of the week. They all seemed to know each other as they stood around.

"Hey baby, you must be Miss Anna. I understand you need our help?" Said one of the black men approaching. Anna had no reluctance. She smiled, kissed him, making sure she could taste the inside of his mouth and then walked over to the other three to introduce herself, leaving her princess standing beside Julia.

Julia turned to Anna's husband and commanded, "Sit!" She pointed to the ground beside a rich leather chair.

"C C Can I I I have a ch ch chair?" He said.

She shook her head, said nothing, and pointed to the ground again. Princess lowered himself to the ground, crossing his legs like a little child in primary school. She sat in the luxurious chair beside him, grabbed his chin to twist his head to look at her instead of his wife.

"So little princess, you're going to watch, no touch and no speak. Do you understand me, little baby princess?" Julia forced his head to swing up and down regardless of his response.

Anna stood speaking to two of the men as the other two went behind her. One of them nibbled her neck, while the other got on his knees and ran his muscular hands up and down her legs. Slowly moving closer and closer to the edge of her shorts. Anna could feel the sexual energy of these four men was massive.

The second man talking to her would not wait for his turn. "Baby, you want to see my cock?" Randomly came from his mouth.

"Oh, I'd love to see it," Anna said, curious to see how well equipped these men were.

Both men removed all their clothes as Anna enjoyed the foreplay the other two were engaged in from behind. She was not disappointed. Neither man needed motivation. They both stood with their cocks already at full attention. She moved forward a single step, took both her right and left hand, and stroked each man.

The other two men helped remove Anna's top, one arm at a time. They undid her shorts and let them fall to the floor. Anna stepped out. One man moved to stimulate her nipples, while the other went back to caressing her still pantyhose encased legs, slowly inching his way on her inner thighs. She spread her legs to allow the young gentleman greater access.

Julia bent over and spoke directly into the princess's ear with a soft seductive voice.

"You love this, don't you, little princess? You want this for your Goddess, don't you?"

He moved his head in agreement, desperate to play with himself as he watched his wife slowly being seduced by four men.

The man caressing Anna's legs had now moved in front

of her, on his knees. His hands clutched her ass, his face fully engorged in between her legs. The two men with their cocks in Anna's hands were kissing her, taking turns on the ears, neck, and mouth. The fourth man was fighting to fill his mouth with her now rock hard nipples.

Princess turned to Julia and could no longer remain silent.

"Thank you so much for this. This is wonderful."

Julia smiled and patted him on the head like he was a dog.

"Little princess, after today, Miss Anna will be a cuck-oldress in every way. You, baby princess, will be her cuck-old. No more back and forth fucking bullshit do I want to hear from your little baby mouth. This is the beginning of the end for you. Do you want that princess? Do you want to be a cuckold forever and ever and ever?" Before he could respond, Julia continued. "Yes, you do. I know your kind."

Anna could overhear the conversation Julia was having with her husband but got lost in the passion of the four men. Her hands gently pulled the two cocks back and forth. She could feel them both throbbing for more. Her mind filled with pleasure, one of the men gently coaxed her to the bed that lay directly in front of Julia and the princess. The other man nudged her to lie down.

Leaning back, two of the men supported her head so her landing was soft and smooth. They created a liberal hole in her pantyhose so she did not need to take them off as they continued to play. This was a request Julia made to them, before Anna and princess's arrival.

Lifting her legs, a new mouth greeted Anna between her legs. This man knew how to stimulate her clit. The steady and constant stimulation back and forth launched her into multiple mini orgasms. Another straddled her with his dark legs on either side of her chest. He grabbed her ponytail and pulled her head forward. His cock danced around her lips, teasing.

Anna licked his head like it was the best lollipop she had ever tasted. He waited only a moment before ramming it down the back of her throat. It stretched her jaw to its limits. She wanted this cock inside.

Princess watched with distressed admiration. Julia took her hand and flicked his caged cock with her index finger.

"You see that? That's a fucking useless piece of shit. Don't you dare deprive Miss Anna with that embarrassment again." Julia said, noticing the fluid dripping out. "Oh, look at that. Hey Anna, your little princess is so happy, he is leaking pre-cum."

Anna heard Julia but could not respond. They engulfed her in pleasure. She wanted more. She wanted more cock everywhere.

All four men had worked themselves into a frenzy of testosterone. The man with his cock in Anna's mouth was the dominant. He stood up and moved the man with his head between her legs. He shifted Anna on her stomach and pulled her backside up. His position was filled instantly with another longer but slimmer cock craving Anna's mouth. His cock dangled towards her lips. She sucked hard.

The other two men made sure Anna was being stimulated in all the right places. Two hands cradling her tits, the other two rubbing her body and her clit. The big black man pulled her ass cheeks apart and guided his cock.

Slowly, gently. His head went in, then out. He was teasing her.

Anna wanted to feel this huge hard cock. She needed it deep inside her. She was going to die if he did not give her more. She wanted more. She plunged backward, forcing his cock deep, deep inside. Every part of her being was about these men. She felt so desired, so incredibly lusted after. She felt like a total slut and was loving every single second of it.

Princess watched his wife being spit-roasted with no mercy. He had never seen such a beautiful sight. It was wonderful. Julia could see he was on the edge of tipping over. She capitalized the moment.

"Stop fighting this, little princess. What your watching feels so good to you right now, doesn't it? It feels so right, doesn't it? So, stop fighting yourself. You know you've already lost the fight. Just accept this. It's the way you want it to be. It's the way it has to be. Miss Anna is your Goddess. She owns your soul. Stop fighting, okay little princess?"

Princess turned to Julia. "Yes, Miss Julia. You are right. It has to be this way. I am a cuckold." He was not embarrassed as the words came out. The freedom of no longer fighting empowered him.

Anna, barely conscious of the dialogue, heard enough to know this was her moment. Following Julia's advice from earlier in the day, she stopped sucking and turned to her husband.

"You are my little fucking princess. DO YOU FUCKING UNDERSTAND ME, BITCH?"

He immediately jumped up on to his knees, crawled to her, and moved in over the bed. The smell of the other men's sex was all over Anna's face. He leaned into her and whispered.

"Yes, my Goddess. You own me. Thank you so much for this. I love you and I'm eternally grateful." He then reached further, kissing her, making sure his tongue roamed the inside of her mouth. He relished the moment before resuming his little princess seat beside Miss Julia.

# CHAPTER ELEVEN

wo hours later, all four men had a turn with Anna. Princess watched with adoring eyes the entire time. Never lifting his eyes from his wife. Julia continuously drew the attention of the little princess to all four bulls and Anna.

Two of the men had tapped out and could no longer keep up with Anna's desires. She was a sexual dynamo with a bottomless need for pleasure. Finally, Julia stood up and walked towards Anna. She placed her hand on Anna's head to get her attention.

"It's time, my love. It's time to seal the deal."

Anna smiled with acknowledgment.

Julia turned back to the man sitting stark naked on the floor, legs crossed and a metal cage around his cock.

"Okay, little princess. Miss Anna needs you on the bed." Julia tapped the bed.

The princess got up and was unsure what was about to happen.

"Good little girl. Don't you think she's been a good little princess, gentlemen?" Julia said as she turned to the two men still fully engorged in Anna's body.

Both men laughed.

"He's a fucking wimp. Look at the fucking loser." One of the two men said.

Julia snapped at the remark. Her face said she was not impressed by the comment.

"Listen, boys. I never want to hear you speak to Anna's husband like that again, if you ever plan on seeing any action with me, her, or any of my other girls. DO YOU FUCKING UNDERSTAND, BOY?"

The action stopped completely.

"Miss Anna can say those things. She should say those things. Even worse. But you keep your fucking mouths shut at all times. You're here to fuck. That's it. That's all, folks. This is about Anna and her princess. You're just the side characters in this little play. You got it?"

All four men responded with a respectful "Yes, Miss Julia."

Julia made a dramatic pause and then went on.

"Okay, which one of you boys' minds Anna's princess sucking your cock for a little bit. It's just a fucking mouth and I'll give you brownie points for future invites."

The two men that had tapped out earlier raised their hands.

Julia turned to Anna. "Okay, Miss Anna. You know what you have to do. Now do it."

Anna turned to her princess. He was shaking his head. The look of desperation was all over his face.

"Please Anna, please. I mean my Goddess. Please. Don't."

For the first time since the day started, Anna felt guilty. She knew her husband well enough to know he desperately did not want to suck another man's cock. Still, the temptation to see how much total control she could have over this man was addictive. She had to kill whatever real man was left inside him. She didn't want her husband to be gay, but she wanted to kill any chance that she would lose this complete domination. She paused as silence fell over the room to see if she could burn the bridge forever.

"My cute little princess, I want you to suck another man's cock. I think it would be really sweet and special if we could both suck a cock at the same time. We can take turns. And then you can help him fuck me. Don't you want that?"

Her husband burst into tears. He had reached his breaking point. He could not cross that line.

"I'm s s s so sorry, Anna. I c c can't."

Julia intercepted the dialogue quickly. She could see Anna was feeling remorse. All the ground they had made could be lost if she did not act.

"Okay, little princess. We were just testing you. You go back and sit in the corner." Julia said, commanding everyone's attention.

She looked at Anna and mouthed the words "we'll talk later".

Anna had lost her mojo and was well on the way to exhaustion. The two men looked at her and did not need to be told. The four men were dressed and out of the basement within minutes.

The princess remained in the corner, now erupting in

tears. The demands were too strong, pushing him over the edge. Passing him a box of tissue, Julia went back to Anna and led her upstairs while the princess mourned.

"Anna, don't think right now. Just don't. He'll get over it. Now, more than ever, you need to keep your own shit together. If he sees you fall apart, this will cause tremendous damage to both of you. Just carry on like your his Goddess. Show little mercy on his disposition."

Anna was emotionally numb. She intuitively knew Julia was right, and that was all she could go on.

"Okay, Julia,"

"But understand Anna, we're not done with this. He needs this back-and-forth headspace to end. So do you! I'm telling you, you need to make this shift final. As it just so happens, I know just the perfect landing spot for this to happen."

"Where? What are you talking about Julia?"

Julia handed Anna a cigarette as she continued.

"Club Cuckoo,"

"What? What the fuck is club cuckoo?" Anna asked.

"Let's just say it's a sort of... training resort. It's a perfect holiday destination the four of us need to go on. It will help both of you so much. Oh, and girl, you and I. Oh My God, I can see us there already. We're gonna have fuuunnnn!"

# WHAT DID YOU THINK?

I am so grateful that you have purchased this book. It means the world to davie and I. If you are enjoying the series thus far, leave a quick review with the book retailer you have purchased it from. It will help me continue making the content that puts a smile on your face and a bump in your panties :)

Toodles. A xo

## ALSO BY ALLORA SINCLAIR

DNA OF A CUCKOLD - THE MISSING LINK

DNA OF A CUCKOLD - HUSBAND EDITION

DNA OF A CUCKOLD - WIFE EDITION

DNA OF A CUCKOLD - ADVANCED COUPLES

THE MENTOR - 15 YEARS EARLIER- Prologue

THE MENTOR 1 - A BAD INFLUENCE

THE MENTOR 3 - COMPLETE INFLUENCE

CUCKOLD ADDICTION - FIGHT IT OR EMBRACE IT?

BAD GIRLS - THE GUIDE TO FEMALE POWER

# ABOUT THE AUTHOR

Allora Sinclair is a happily married 40 year old mom. She and her loving cuckold husband Dave (davie) have been in a cuckold marriage for over seven years and she has now decided  to start documenting their journey. If Allora is not found at her computer, or out shopping for a new pair of shoes, she is usually found in the caring arms of davie or embraced in ecstasy with one of her favorite bulls. She has done a series of non-fiction books to help couples navigate their way through the heavily distorted life of being a cuckold couple. She is now working on a series of fiction books that are loosely based on some of their real-life adventures. This story would be one.